a cheer

FOR THE YEAR

WRITTEN BY RAVEN HOWELL

ILLUSTRATED BY MEREDITH MESSINGER

Summary: A Cheer for the Year offers a poetic calendar of holiday
treats, the feeling you get when a friend presses a box of decadent
chocolates in your hands, and you didn't even know that's what you
were missing.

Author/poet Raven Howell lights sparklers, flips pancakes and dances
us merrily through the year while illustrator Meredith Fern's paper
cut-outs create the friendly, imaginative, and expressive home for each
verse.

Clear Fork Publishing
P.O. Box 870
102 S. Swenson
Stamford, Texas 79553
(325)773-5550
www.clearforkpublishing.com

Printed and Bound in the United States of America.

ISBN - 978-1-950169-34-4

Acknowledgement/Dedication

These holiday poems are inspired by the special opportunities we have to celebrate treasured traditions. I hope that my verse triggers memories of happy occasions passed and holiday fun to still look forward to and honor.

In the spirit of our book's dedication, I wish the excitement, anticipation and bright celebration of many more festivities. May you share your child-like heart with "cheer". - Raven

For my family, my year round cheer. - Meredith

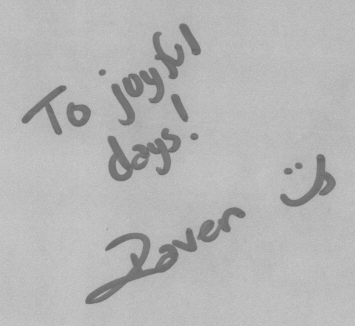

NEW YEAR'S

New Year's Day,
Frizzle frazzle,
Shiver, shimmer,
Razzle dazzle.
Icicles of pointy picks,
Promises of snow that sticks.
Sledding downhill,
Zooming by
New Year's snowmen
Waving "Hi!"

CELEBRATE MARTIN LUTHER KING JR. DAY!

Steadfast in justice
Fervently loyal
Noble, majestic
King, a true *royal*.

Question to Groundhog

Mushy rain, slushy snow,
It's neither wet nor frozen.
A very frigid sludgy mess
The gray-streaked clouds have chosen.

It spatters down, hits the ground
It's sleet, and sleet is sloppy.
I dropped my homework paper.
It made it moist and floppy.

A snowman? A snowball?
I can't make a thing.
Groundhog, please just tell me
Is it winter still, or spring?

Oh, Valentine!

Oh, Valentine, you've so much fur!
Your green eyes glow,
You like to purr.

If there's a ray of sun, you nap,
So quick to find a cozy lap.

Oh, Valentine, you're warm and sweet,
And always ready for a treat!

TO GEORGE WASHINGTON

ON PRESIDENT'S DAY

I know you helped care for your sister and brothers,

Augustine was your dad, Mary, your mother.

I know you read books and liked music and art,

I learned you were brave, stoic and smart.

But for some time now it's been niggling me:

Did you really chop down

Your dad's cherry tree?

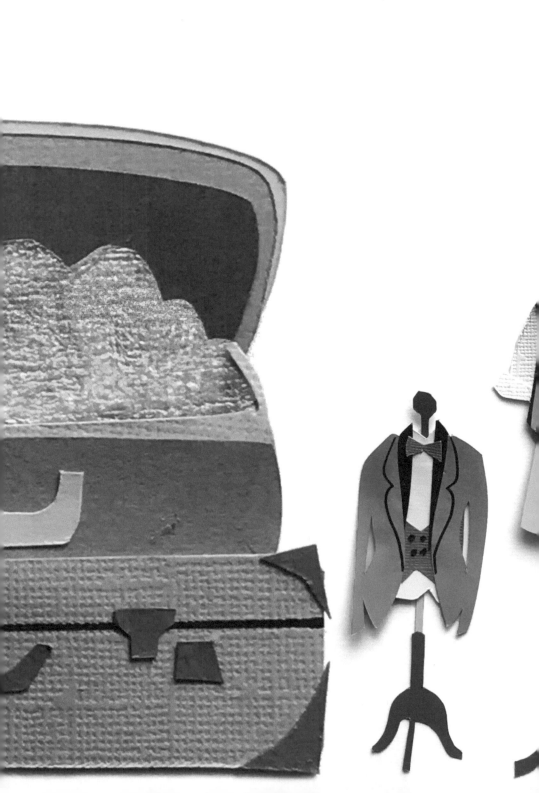

WEAR GREEN FOR ST. PATTY'S!

You'll find the Leprechaun dresses in green,
In matted hue or shiny sheen,
Sundays emerald, Mondays lime,
Tuesdays silver green like thyme,
Forest, aqua, even teal,
Puckered sour apple zeal.

Though green appears to be his zest,
It's gleaming gold he likes the best!

ARBOR DAY
(EARTH CELEBRATION)

Our class observes
The trees that grow.
On every branch
We tie a bow.

We plant a sapling
By the gate.
It's Arbor Day —
Let's celebrate!

Easter Sunday, Breakfast

Eggs are scrambled,
Eggs are fried.
We crack them
On their sunny side.

Eggs are boiled
As you please,
And cooked as omelets
With some cheese.

An Easter gift!
And packaged well —
A meal tucked in
A chicken shell.

On Mother's Day

I chose a dandelion,
Found shade where violets grew.

I picked a yellow buttercup
And purple clover, too.

I gave them to my mother —
And got a kiss and hug.

We laughed when we found this bouquet
Came with a ladybug!

A Memorial Parade

Clarinets,
A brass trombone,
Drums are beating,
Tubas moan.

We march in time
And proudly greet
Friends who cheer
Along the street.

A bright salute
And flags held high
Commemorate
Heroes gone by.

On Father's Day

I mixed and stirred the pancake dough
Then poured it out, steady and slow,
Which made the bubbling batter brown
'Til we turned the pancake upside down.

Then Dad held the pan
And gave it a shake,
Saying, "This is how you flip a pancake",
But the pancake flew too high I think -
It landed on the ceiling above the sink!

4TH OF JULY

July was made for lemonade,
For sparklers, pops, and a parade,
For fireworks crackling the sky,
For climbing trees, and swinging high!

GOING ON A PICNIC
(AMERICAN FAMILY DAY)

Dad gets the kite, Mom packs the lunch,
I grab the tablecloth and the fruit punch.
Little Baby Sue brings her great big smile,
And the day fetches sunshine
Mile after mile.

When Labor Day Comes

Autumn licks its lips,
Puts ice on a breeze
And sips slowly.
Plucks a flower,

Frosts a leaf,
Chews a sun ray
Between its teeth,
Considers a pine —
Doesn't like its flavor.
Heads North,
Toasting green grass
Until it turns brown,
Eating summer
Out of our town.

SCHOOL PLAY

We learn about explorers
From our history book.
We memorize the poems about
Courageous trips they took.

Scenes are set, and lines rehearsed
Echo backstage rooms.
Gabe is good at making props,
Our parents make costumes.

Cardboard cut out wagons,
Boats, and rail cars, too
Are strapped around the shoulders
Of Peter, Jake, and Lou.

We're well prepared, the school doors open,
Seats all quickly fill.
The audience cheers loud and claps,
Our racing heartbeats thrill!

And Grace in her best singing voice
Strikes up a lively tune
While railways hum, and ships set sail
By light of star and moon (played by Laura and Danny).

To Grandma
On Grandparent's Day

Grandma, thanks for the sweater you knit,
But I gave it to Jen — it's a much better fit.
It's not that I don't like the bright orange weave
Or the pom-poms sewn on to the flowery sleeves.
It's just that I think that the trouble's my tummy
It reminds me -your chocolate chip cookies are yummy!
Though Mom made the usual angel food cake
Gran, nothing's as good as those cookies you bake!

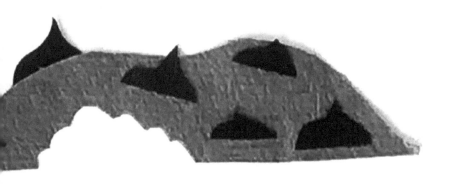

WHEN LEAVES CHANGE

When leaves change to yellow from green,
To the prettiest colors you've seen
I parade my costume
In witch hat and broom
Because soon it will be Halloween!

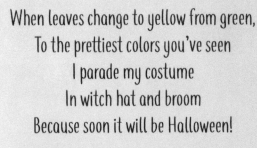

A DEVILISH DIAMANTE

Halloween
Ghoulish, ghostly
Carving, creeping, cackling
Doorbells ringing, black cats hackling
Haunting, hooting, howling
Chilly, thrill-y
Boo!

Our Thanksgiving

My sister argues, mom's stressed out,
Dad seems tired, both twins shout.
The dog barks loudly, quite upset,
Our cat's just trouble - bedding's wet!
We set the table, plates and dishes,
Give our thanks, and share well wishes.
The turkey's out- the chaos past,
Thanksgiving in our home at last!

SURPRISE!
(The Day After Thanksgiving)

We stop to choose an evergreen
Though winter cold winds blow.
They dance and swirl, and decorate
Our Christmas tree with snow.

Latkes!

Grab that apron from the peg,
Mix potatoes, onion, egg.

The pan is oiled, patties down,
Fry both sides until they brown.

Add applesauce, fresh and sweet,
Blessings first — and then we eat!

KWANZAA

My family gathers
With neighbors and friends
To honor our culture
When autumn ends.

Black for the color,
Green for the land,
Red for the struggle
For freedom to stand.

Colorful baskets
And African art;
Bowlfuls of fresh fruit,
Joy in the heart.

CHRISTMAS

Green and red
Gingerbread
Snowmen grinning
Tree trimming
Bells jingling
Toes tingling
Presents wrapped
Gifts stacked
Silent night
Angel's flight
Turkey roasting
Christmas toasting.

WELCOME BACK!

Another New Year -
Welcome home!
Days in hundreds, honeycombed,

Months, bright eggs about to hatch-
A dozen
With seasons to match.

The coming year-
What will it bring?
Let's sound a cheer
And dance and sing!

CHILDREN'S HOLIDAY ACTIVITY

I engage you to create your own holiday. What would it be called? How would you commemorate it? Write a story or poem to explain or describe it. When would your holiday be celebrated? What would it look like? Draw a picture.

Feel free to connect should you want to let me in on it!
www.ravenhowell.com

With year round inspiration, Raven Howell writes books and poetry for children. She enjoys sharing book presentations and kids' workshops, visiting schools, classrooms and libraries. Raven is the Creative & Publishing Advisor for RedClover Reader and writes The Book Bug column for Story Monsters Ink magazine.

She delights in all holiday celebrations, and finds Halloween a particularly mischievous, mysterious, sugar-inducing event.

Also by Raven Howell, available through Clear Fork Publishing:
Shimmer, Songs of Night (illustrated by Carina Povarchik)
Glimmer, Sing of Sun! (illustrated by Carina Povarchik)

Meredith Fern Messinger is a Boise based illustrator and designer who loves to draw, cut, sew, make and create. She lives happily with her husband, two year old daughter, newborn son, two Siamese cats, and a goldfish.

CPSIA information can be obtained
at www.ICGtesting.com
Printed in the USA
BVHW021822171220
595870BV00015B/91/J

9 781950 169344